Human minds are magical in the way they can combine the arts of storytelling and illustration to create something more powerful than either the tale or the pictures by themselves. We have worked to combine beautiful imagery with intriguingly told tales, as we sought to create such magic. We hope you will agree that we have, in our own way, produced something magical.

Tales From Other Realms

Stories of the Mundane World

A Dedication

I am grateful for the inspiring example of my daughter Jennifer; the confidence gained from studying/working with Tommy Osuna; and the encouragement of friends like Brian Whelan, Patrick Doran, Jeff Carr, Paul Waltz and John Hatton.

A special thanks to my friend and partner Tad Gallaugher, who exhausted himself time after time in his unquenchable desire to push this project to the highest possible level, and who generously invited me to share in his creative process.

Eldon James Kraft

I want to thank all my Teachers, Professors, Instructors, Directors, Colleagues and anyone who has exchanged or collaborated on creative possibilities with me for they all helped bring me to this level of my craft.

A huge thanks to Eldon James Kraft for creating these stories of adventure and fantasy and encouraging me to illustrate this book.

A very special thanks to Frank Hoflelt: You always pushed me in a positive direction.

My most sincere thanks to Alan Gough and his wife Joy for their interest in nurturing me and to Alan for the guidance he provided to help me develop my talent throughout my high school and college years.

T.N. GALLAUGHER

ISBN 979-8-218-00199-5

Library of Congress Control Number: 2022942615

Copyright©2022 by Eldon James Kraft and Tad Gallaugher • Printed by

Quotes on divider pages and final page are taken from the song: Truth and Fantasy, Richard Keelan, Perth County Conspiracy – Does Not Exist, Columbia Records, 1970

An Odd Collection of Very, Very Short Stories

Written by **Eldon James Kraft** ▲ Illustrated by **T.N. Gallaugher**

The Customer is Always Right

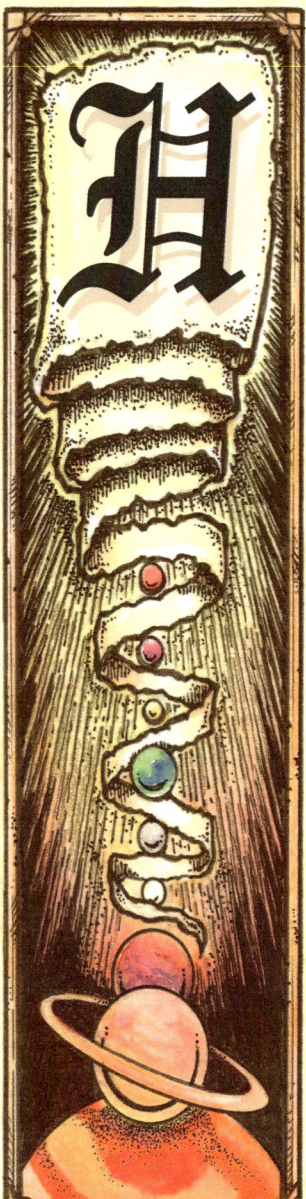

He was a small man sitting on a tall stool on the business side of a counter at a local cable company office. He exuded an air of self-importance, barely concealed impatience and condescension.

Quite amazing considering that he was, in fact, hanging on the very bottom of a corporate ladder that he would most likely never climb.

A tall elderly gentleman entered the lobby. He approached the clerks's counter in a voluminous black great coat. "How may I help you" the clerk asked in a disinterested tone. The gentleman reached inside his coat and withdrew a wallet. "I've come to pay my cable bill" he spoke quietly but clearly. "Didn't I tell you last time about paying online or using the app?" the clerk hissed. "Yes you did" the man answered calmly, "but I prefer to pay in person".

The clerk seemed to inflate a bit as he sneered "Well if you do so next month there will be a five dollar service charge for the privilege". The old man was silent while the clerk took his credit card and processed the transaction. When the man had signed the charge and received his receipt and card back the clerk turned away.

But the man did not leave. As he reached into another pocket of his great coat he spoke to the clerk "I have something here I think you must see" and he laid a clear glass globe on the counter. The clerk's bored expression disappeared as he turned and saw the globe. As he stared at the ball ill-defined shapes in vivid colors began to form. They seemed to intermingle without blending. Royal purples, acid greens, electric blues and violent pinks. They danced about hinting at new forms but never actually coalescing.

The "Mage" smiled as his finger drew a line line in the air between the ball and clerk's forhead. A band of light containing all the colors followed that line until it reached the forehead and then it proceeded to completely envelop the clerk's body. The clerk cried out unintelligibly once and then fell silent. The light began to shrink into a small ball which retraced its path to the globe. The clerk's stool sat empty.

The supervisor, having heard the clerk's last exclamation, entered the area behind the counter and noted his clerk had apparently abandoned his station. He looked up as the bell rang signaling the door opening. He noticed a tall elderly gentleman in a large black great coat departing the building. He was startled when he noticed a small capuchin monkey clinging to the man's shoulder. The monkey looked imploringly at the supervisor as the door closed and the office was once again empty.

He heard the man speaking but he could not tear his glance from the show before him. The man's voice seemed to come from a great distance yet his words were crystal clear. "It seems your physical development has greatly outpaced your spiritual growth. But I have a cure for that."

An Odd Collection of Very, Very Short Stories

The Customer is Always Right

Reincarnation

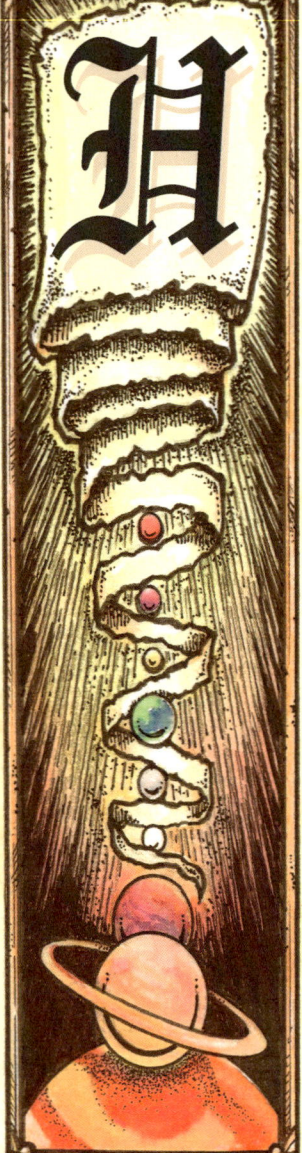

He had been himself in a previous life-time. In fact, he had been himself in many previous lifetimes. Never once was he anyone or anything else.

He remembered the last dozen or so fairly well and little bits of the dozen before that. Sometimes he would recognize someone he'd been alive with before. He always greeted them enthusiastically. They inevitably found his friendliness a bit odd; however they usually seemed to feel some kind of connection to him.

He never met anyone like him; at least he didn't think he had. On rare occasions he would notice someone observing him with a curious expression. He wondered if it was someone like him who had remained themselves through multiple incarnations. But he never dared risk exposing himself. After all, how crazy would he sound to the average person who had no knowledge of their own reincarnation?

One day he was ambling along the boardwalk headed for the pier when he noticed a woman about ten feet ahead of him.Somthing about her seemed familiar, even from behind. As they got to the pier she turned, providing him with a profile view. He was now sure he'd known her in a past life. He dove into his memories as he trailed behind her. As he observed more of her mannerisms he became increasingly certain. Then he remembered.

It had been two or three cycles back. They had come together quickly and passionately. It had been like a Hollywood romance right up through the night of the engagement party. He had an early business trip the next day so he dropped her off at her apartment. He never saw her again.

That had been the defining event of that cycle. He never fully recovered until the in-between time. Now he realized he still hadn't fully recovered. He strode over and placed himself in her path. "What happened?" he barked. He watched confusion, recognition and affection appear in her eyes in a fraction of a second. She assumed a bland expression and asked "What are you talking about?" As he stared her face seemed to collapse, a sob rose from her throat and she fell into his arms.

"What happened?" he repeated much more softly. She pulled a kleenex out of her purse, dried her eyes and said, "We need to find a private place to talk. I've rented a cottage 3 blocks off the beach. Come there with me and I'll answer your questions." He walked beside her in a daze until they entered a one bedroom beach house. He faced her, ready to demand an explanation, but she held up a hand and began to speak. "There's more to this reality we inhabit than you know. Most of the people around us are sleepers, they begin each cycle with no memory of their past. A tiny percentage is different. They call themselves sentients. Over the course of many cycles they have evolved into beings capable of manipulating space-time." They seek

to guide the sleeper's evolution to an eventual sentient existence.

As she paused he broke in, "What does this have to do with you leaving me at the altar so to speak?" A weary smile formed on her face "I was kidnapped by sentients." She waved off his questioning look "the smallest percentage of our collective being is people like you and I. We are neither sleepers nor sentients. This worries them. When it looked like the two of us might produce offspring they felt compelled to act. I was kidnapped and placed in the in-between time."

He had watched her intently as she spoke and he found her credible. "Are there others like us?" and she nodded. She smiled and said "You know I've had a few more cycles than you. I've picked up a few tricks." He raised an eyebrow. She clapped her hands together and her clothes disappeared. "Wow" he exclaimed "you're beautiful; different but beautiful". "You prefer the woman you were engaged to?" she snapped her finger and became his former fiancé. As he approached her, the expression on her face changed to one of dismay "They've found us" Then her form began to waver. "We cycle on the same schedule. Look for me next cycle" Her form dissolved and he was alone.

In the Balance

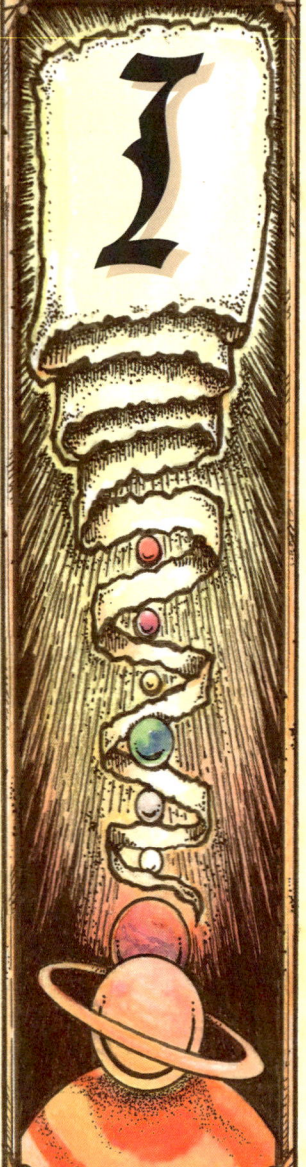

I t was in a small sound-proofed room with padded walls and a door that locked from the inside. It was my second day of what might be anywhere from 3 to 7 in total.

I was in the restoration-time seeking equanimity after killing a very good man in the name of "The Balance." Our rules said I should not be disturbed and should be left alone until I emerged of my own will.

The light over the door came on. It meant I should open the door. Only the master of our order could direct such a thing. In more than two decades as an agent of the order this had never happened to me. Nor had I ever heard of it happening to another agent. In a foul temper

I slid back the cover of a small opening in the door and saw a young acolyte standing there. "What?" I snarled. "The Master requires your presence in his study" he replied. "You are permitted time to return to your apartment and make yourself presentable."

A bit less than an hour later I knocked on the study door. "Come in Number 2" I heard the worry in his voice. "What is the matter, Abbot?" I began, "This is most unusual". "These are unusual times" was his mild reply as he motioned for me to be seated across the desk from him. He poured a dark amber liquid into a pair of crystal glasses and handed one to me "This may help you, with your unsettled state." "And you, I said" still not mollified "are you also unsettled?" "Indeed" was all he said but his expression was dour.

He took a sip and spoke "A new holy one has arisen." "Somewhere in the Middle East no doubt," was my reply. "Aye," his face contorted in a mirthless grin. "But this time it is different than any occasion recorded in our annals," he continued. "It seems everything we've worked for through the millennia is now at risk." he paused. "His sphere of influence is large and growing. For a hundred miles around all are of his spirit; in the next hundred miles he is universally venerated. Regimes two to three hundred miles away consider him an ally to protect," The Abbot shook off

his head. "There have been others in the past that were equal powers for good. But their impact was more diffused geographically which left them more open to attack." Staring at the abbot I spoke "How do you imagine an agent like I could get close enough to strike and how might I survive?"

He took another sip of his drink and began, "In your current unrestored condition good and evil are at war within you. If you nurture the evil, let it create the devious plan and let it use the good as a disguise to hide behind…you might reach him."

I drained the rest of my glass and asked, "And as to my survival?" All he offered by way of an answer was a sorrowful stare. "Then you do not anticipate my survival?" He nodded. "All our studies suggest that should he continue to expand he will eventually call into being an equally pure and potent evil to balance against him. The outcome of such a titanic clash cannot be predicted."

I stood abruptly "I will of course honor my oath and obey your directive. I have two more questions before I leave you to begin my preparations." He stared into his glass and without looking up said "Yes?" I turned my back to him "Where is Number 1 and why was this task not assigned to him?" The resulting silence seemed to last a very long time. "It was assigned to him. He resides now with the holy one."

There was nothing more to say. I stopped briefly at my apartment to collect my travel gear and was on the road within the hour.

Keepsake

Some of the more prominent nobles of the western march had complained of the depredations of a young dragon. So here he was leading a company of twenty, 10 lancers and 10 archers, about an hour's ride west of the capital.

The kingdom had been at peace for a decade so his company was made up entirely of young untested men. It turned out he was right to be leery of their likely performance. The party was approaching the ruin of centuries old castle.

The ruins sat on a hilltop which afforded them an unobstructed view for miles in every direction. As they approached the ruins a shift in the wind brought the stench of a nearby dragon to their noses. As they crested the hill the ruins sat upon they saw a young female dragon sleeping in a bed dug out of the hillside a hundred feet below. He ordered the men to hold but like berserkers they charged down the hill. The dragon never had a chance. So many arrows and lances pierced its breast that it died sleeping.

The men began celebrating and congratulating each other. Above them on the hilltop he heard a distant keening. As it grew louder he found the direction it came from and looked to the north. In the distance but drawing rapidly nearer he spotted what looked to be a mature dragon. The men didn't hear his cries so he sounded the battle horn and pointed to the north sky. Some of the men saw the dragon and began to react but it looked to be too few and decidedly too late.

He rode his horse through the ruins and dismounted at the door to the keep which he knew to be solid from prior explorations. He grabbed his kit and his weapons and tossed them into the old armory. He swatted his horse's ass which sent him running. Hopefully he would distract the dragon and maybe even escape. His ears were filled with the screams of the men and the bellowing of the dragon. He closed the door and surveyed the room. It was lit by a narrow ceiling vent and he could see piles of wreckage from the collapse of the second floor. He spied a piece of a floor joist under some of the rubble. It was a ten by ten wood beam that appeared long enough to use as a cross bar for the door. Driven by his fear of the dragon he managed to drag the joist to the door, lift it and place in the iron holders secured to the wall on each side of the door.

As the adrenaline ebbed he leaned against a wall and took stock of his situation. He had light while the sun was up via the ceiling vent. He saw rusted pipe protruding from the wall above a carved basin. It was dripping steadily so he had water; though the quality might be suspect. The bottom of the basin sloped down from where the pipe dripped to a partially clogged drain so it could function as his latrine. In his kit he had two apples, a small block of cheese and one piece of hardtack. He was armed with a short sword and a crossbow. The dragon could not reach him and he could survive several days in good condition. He thought it had been well into the afternoon when they came upon the dragon. He felt exhaustion pulling him down. Making a pillow of his cape he lay down and slept.

He awoke gagging and heard the bass grumbling from the other side of the door. The dragon had found him. It was night and the light from a waning quarter moon allowed him to pace but not to search the room. He thought about how he might kill the dragon, given an opportunity. A dragon's throat was less protected by the leathery scales that covered most of its body. A large enough blade plunged deeply into that soft spot would kill it, but how could that be accomplished? He considered his weapons. The blade of the short sword might suffice if sunk with sufficient force. The cross bow could deliver a bolt with sufficient force but the bolts were too thin and short.

As he paced the room it occurred to him that he might combine his two weapons. If he removed the hilt and the guard from the sword he might attach it to a bolt and create a weapon adequate to the task. Delivering such a blow was another problem but one thing at a time. An hour later the sky had brightened enough to begin work. He used his dirk to separate the hilt from the tang of the blade. With that done the hilt slid cleanly off. He removed the remaining food from his kit and began the task of slicing the leather bag into strips. He cleaned the fletching off the bolt. When these tasks were complete he soaked each strip in the basin before tying them around the tang of the sword and the shaft of the bolt. The two parts were bound together by a dozen strips when he finished. It was late afternoon judged by the light in the room. He ate a few slices of apple, a piece of hardtack and half of the cheese. Come morning he's see if the binding was tight enough and, if it was, he'd try to devise a strategy for how to use the weapon that had at least a small chance of success. He remade his pillow, lay down and slept.

When he awoke the next day the smell and sounds of the dragon were still just outside his door. He checked the strength of the joining of his blade and the bolt and found it to be satisfactory. He allowed himself a drink of water and two slices of apple before he began examining the contents of the room hoping for inspiration. The open area of the floor contained nothing useful; only bits of debris. Each corner of the room contained a small pile of rubble. He took a length of iron he had found near the basin and started to carefully scatter each debris pile. A few hours later he considered a small group of objects spread out in the light of the vent. Perhaps the second floor had been the treasury he thought.

Although the castle had been looted many times since its fall he still had found several objects of some value. A few gold coins of the type that had a hole in the center, a couple of rings set with what looked to be semi-precious stones and a silver jeweled broach. As he contemplated the objects before him a plan began to take shape in his mind; If he washed away the

grime on the objects they would sparkle and shine. Dragons, as all know, like things that sparkle and shine. He smiled as he set to work cleaning.

By midafternoon the objects were ready; that is, they were as clean as he could get them. He pulled another bolt out of the quiver. He walked over and stood below the vent. It was narrow and short but he thought he could he could fire a bolt through it with an angle between five and ten degrees. At maximum force, and with the added weight of the objects he'd found he figured the bolt might come to ground about a hundred yards away. He'd have to risk removing the crossbar before he fired the lure but, if all went as planned, he'd have a minute or two to open the door and position himself for a shot when the dragon turned to strike.

By the time he finished assembling the lure, using the last of the leather strips, the sun was setting. He ate the last of the cheese and hardtack leaving him with a single apple for breakfast. He took a drink and remade his "bed". He lay awake for many hours mentally rehearsing the execution of the plan he had made. The last thing he remembered was noting the faint illumination of the moonlight, and then he was asleep.

He woke early at first light. He ate half of the apple and took a drink before getting to work. He hoped the dragon might sleep through any noise he made removing the crossbar and he thought it'd be best to take the shot with the sun low enough to be blocked from blinding him by the keep. He wolfed down the remaining apple and took a drink, wondering if this was to be his last meal. Inch by inch he slid the crossbar through the iron holders. When one end was almost clear he lifted it slowly and lowered it to the ground. Then he lifted the other end and pivoted until the crossbar was ninety degrees to the door. He grunted as he lifted the end nearer the door and moved it just enough that the door could open.

He loaded the lure into the crossbow and positioned what he hoped would be the killing weapon next to the door. So far all was well but the next stage could easily end very badly. The dragon had to be awake if the lure was to have any chance of success. He stomped about the room banging the walls with length of iron he'd used in his search of the room. If the dragon moved against the door it would open and he'd be doomed. He detected no movement but a low grumble let him know the creature was awake.

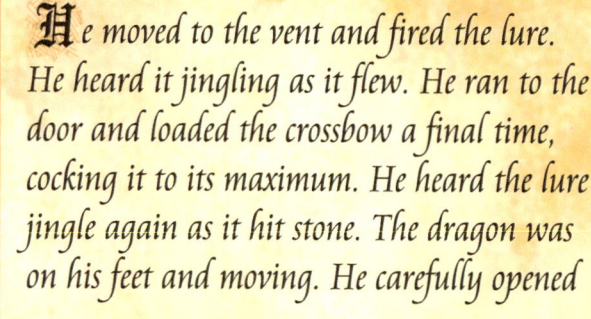

He moved to the vent and fired the lure. He heard it jingling as it flew. He ran to the door and loaded the crossbow a final time, cocking it to its maximum. He heard the lure jingle again as it hit stone. The dragon was on his feet and moving. He carefully opened

the door and slipped through. The dragon was a bit less than a hundred yards away with his back to the man. He called out to the dragon and it turned toward him. As it gathered itself to pounce he fired at the clear white patch below the dragon's chin; aiming high to allow for the extra weight.

The improvised bolt plunged deep into the dragon's vitals. The dragon bellowed and he clutched at his throat. The man returned to the keep to wait out the death throes of the beast. He didn't bother to close the door. His laughter sounded grim but his heart soared as he imagined what now lay in his future and how much more he would savor it after what he'd survived.

He decided he would go and collect the lure before he began the long walk home.

The Uses of Magic

The wizard Ementhor paced about his study. A pentangle was inlaid into the floor in the center of the room. Every time he paced across it the symbol would begin to come to life; rising out of the floor as if to embrace him and falling back as he completed his traverse.

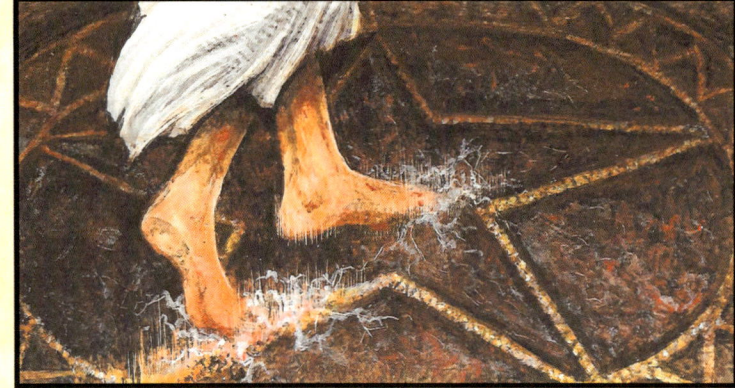

He was disturbed to find that his thoughts seemed to be anchored in the distant past. "It's been half of a millennia since I've had the opportunity to gather with others of my kind," he thought; "Over a century since my last sighting of any sort of magical being!"

It had begun with that young Aramaic speaking prophet advancing the notion of a single deity. "We could have lived with that," he thought, "but his followers insisted that any other powers were evil and needed to be destroyed." It had them taken centuries but gradually people stopped believing in magic and magical beings.

If they retained any belief they viewed magic with fear and suspicion. Numbers lost their magic, becoming mere tools for managing quantities and distances. Alchemy degraded into chemistry. More and more, only things that could be seen and measured were considered real. "I've heard enough about the so called scientific method to last me three lifetimes!" he thought. He halted his pacing in front of his desk and considered the grimoire that lay upon it. It was opened to the final pages. The letters had a soft glow to them. It was the oldest grimoire that he possessed and every other one he'd acquired through the centuries warned against it. They cautioned against using it in general and against the final spell in particular. There were grim warnings about the fate of those who tried to work that final spell. "But how could anyone have known the particulars to warn of," he thought, "if, as they said, none survived the working of that charm." He spoke to his familiar as if the capuchin might answer "Am I ready to risk everything for a chance to escape this dreary plane and find a richer fabric of being like to the one I was born into?"

For that was the promise of the grimoire: an enchantment to turn his Pentangle into a vehicle that would allow him to travel to other planes governed by other laws. He knew he must chance it. To continue this existence seemed unendurable. He had studied the spell so often that all the instructions and chants were engraved in his mind. The book said he could take nothing with him. He shed his cloak and draped it over the back of his chair. As he began to unbutton his shirt a voice sounded in his head, "What about me?" He paused and looked at his familiar. After a brief hesitation he pointed a finger at the creature. A bolt of soft green light shot to the capuchin and enveloped it. The light shrank down

to a small ball which accelerated out of the study. "Thank ..." echoed in the wizard's head as the ball disappeared.

The wizard resumed disrobing. Last of all he took of his most potent talisman: The ring that had been on his right index finger since his earliest years. He was completely naked and could not remember ever feeling so defenseless. He strode to the center of the pentangle. His eyes traced a slow lingering path around the study. Finally he closed his eyes and began the chant. As he began he felt the breeze stirring against his face. Each time he completed a stanza the wind grew in strength. He lost track of time as he continued; stanza after stanza. Toward the end he had to fight for breath. He finished the spell in gale and fell to the floor; too exhausted to do anything but sleep.

He didn't know how long he'd slept but he awakened lying on the floor of a vast hall. The hall was illuminated by a soft light which had no obvious source. Surprisingly he was dressed in the clothes he'd stripped off in his study; his ring was on his finger and his staff lay by him. Standing up, he saw before him a wall of doors arcing away from him in both directions.

He knew he must pass through one of them but how to decide? He reasoned that he must trust that the spell had brought him to the proper place in the massive hall. As he considered the doors directly in front of him he noticed that one door drew his eye more than any of the others. He approached it and as he turned the knob there was a blinding flash of light and a thunder clap that knocked him over. When his senses returned he noticed that he was lying on grass. He opened his eyes upon a curious wood nymph staring down at him.

bout that same time something odd happened in a shopping mall on the plane the wizard had just departed. A recently remodeled storefront had been converted to cell phone sales from its previous use by a local communications company. The customers and staff heard a sound like a thunderclap accompanied by a blaze of light.

hey all shielded their eyes and when they chanced to look they saw a puzzled looking young man standing in their midst. The one closest to him thought he said " …you sir." before collapsing to the floor in a faint.

The Best Laugh

e were a few hours north of the Grand Bahama Island on an eastward tack making for the Port of Charleston in the Carolinas. We were making fair headway with a fresh breeze when a gunshot sounded off to starboard.

Shortly after, the seaman standing watch in the crow's nest called down "unknown party 4 points starboard." I picked up the spyglass and oriented it in the approximate direction. After a moment I spotted a modestly dressed white man on the shore of a nearby islet waving his arms in an exaggerated manner. He didn't look as much like a marooned man so much as an actor portraying a marooned man.

I put aside my misgivings and called out to the First Mate, "Assemble a landing party, Rodgers. Launch the gig and go collect this fellow." I ordered the helmsmen to come about into the wind. It took nearly an hour for the party to row ashore, collect the fellow and return to the ship. After the party was aboard and the gig was stowed I ordered that Rodgers should bring the man to me to be interviewed. Before I could speak he thanked me profusely in a deferential manner. And yet, there was something in his eyes and bearing that suggested command rather than deference.

"Pray tell good fellow," I spoke, "what is your name and how did you come to be in such straits?" The man looked down for a moment and raising his head he fixed his eyes on me "They call me Jimmy, good sir" he showed

a quick smile and paused a moment "I met a party while drinking ashore on Grand Bahama several days past. They planned to rent a cutter and explore the area on the morrow. They said their nautical experience was limited and offered to pay if I would captain the excursion. I was agreeable and a price was settled." He stopped and his pause dragged on "What then, my man?" I interjected. "Your pardon, good sir, but talking is thirsty work and I was short on water on that islet." He looked at me hopefully. "Have someone fetch the fellow a dram, Rodgers" I said as he smiled in what I took for gratitude.

He threw down the dram, briefly closed his eyes and began again "We met at the ship around two bells forenoon and quickly got underway. We coasted until the sun was high and then found a shady cove with a good beach. We tied the cutter off to a palm and took our supplies ashore. After some swimming and a good meal we reboarded and departed the cove. We'd been tacking a short time when a storm like I'd never experienced before descended upon us. In a few minutes we went from gentle to fresh breezes. A few more and the winds were near gale force. The storm drove the cutter before it to the northwest. I fought the rudder so intently I could not say when the members of the

party were lost. After what felt like a lifetime the boat broke up on the beach where you found me. I managed to crawl beyond the waves' reach and passed out. I woke alone as you found me." I still felt a distrust of this man but he stood firm under my stare "Rodgers, have one of the men show Jimmy to a berth so that he may rest and recover his strength. But first sir, I'll have your blunderbuss to lock up with the other firearms. It will be returned to you when you are put ashore." His eyes blazed briefly but he quickly regained his calm. "As you wish Captain." He handed me the weapon and disappeared below deck.

Our progress over the next few days was fair, though slower than I would have liked. I was eager to be quit of our unwanted passenger. I'd caught Rodgers staring at me with a thoughtful expression on several occasions.

Twice I caught two of his more querulous friends among the crew looking at me with ill-disguised hostility. I suspected that Jimmy was stirring up dissatisfaction in the crew quarters. Having been nearly two decades at sea and seven years a captain I understood the signs and prepared myself for the possibility of mutiny.

Late on the third day since we'd acquired our guest I considered allies. The cabin boys, James and William were in their mid-teens. Strong young men I felt to be trustworthy. I resolved to speak with them in the morning. Continuing my preparations I gathered the great coat I sometimes wore on deck. Both the left and right front panels had holsters capable of holding a blunderbuss sewn in just below waist level. The coat had ample volume so that the full holsters would not be easily detectable. I took two of the weapons from the armory, prepared them, placed them in the holsters and hung the coat by the locked cabin door. It was late by then and I decided to put off my entries in the ship's log until morning. I was asleep as soon as my head hit the pillow.

I woke early and got to work on the log book. It was 3 bells forenoon when I heard an emphatic knocking on my door. Rodgers called out "There's been an accident, Sir." I thought I detected a false note in his voice so I took the time to slip into my great coat while I replied "Just a moment." I unlocked and opened the door to find a small party gathered in a semicircle on the deck outside my door. In the first rank stood Jimmy holding a cutlass along with Rodgers and his two ruffian friends. The mate and his cronies carried belaying pins. Perhaps a third of the crew was arrayed behind them but, truth to tell, they looked more like onlookers than mutineers.

Not surprisingly it was Jimmy who broke the silence "I'm sorry to have to repay your kindness in this manner but I'm afraid we must have your ship Captain."

As he stepped forward I took a step to meet him, reached my right hand into my coat and whipped out a blunderbuss.

The look on his face was priceless as I grasped the weapon with both hands, placed the barrel on his chest and fired.

I dropped the blunderbuss in my right hand as he fell to the deck. Reaching my left hand into the coat I withdrew the second blunderbuss, grasped it in two hands and leveled it at Rodgers and company. "This one's loaded with shot" I said smiling "Are there any others here who wish to dispute my captaincy?"

The second rank of supposed mutineers had dispersed at the shot which dropped Jimmy. "Captain—" Rodgers stuttered but I waved him to silence. "I have a proposal for you three, but first I want your friends placed in the brig." I offered "You still hold the key so you may clearly free them if you aren't amenable to what you hear on your return." After a brief whispered conference the three of them headed to the brig. Ever cautious, I took the opportunity to reload the blunderbuss.

When Rodgers returned I spoke immediately "Here is what I propose. For the few days left to reach Charleston you shall continue as First Mate and your companions shall remain locked in the brig. Upon docking I will refrain from reporting the three of you to the authorities. You will disembark with half the pay you would have earned if you had completed the journey and your friends shall each receive a third. What say you?" Rodgers stared at me for a moment "I suppose a letter of recommendation is out the question," he said with an embarrassed grin. I shook my head in disgust. "Very well," he stammered, "It shall be as you say."

"Right, then" I nodded, "have the sailmaker sew yon Jimmy up in a sack. Then place him someplace where the winds will take the stench away. "Have the cabin boys report to me

"Straight away". While I awaited the lads, I replaced the blunderbusses in the armory and withdrew a pair of musketoons. I was just finished loading the weapons when the boys knocked on the door. "We've just avoided a near mutiny as you are no doubt aware." The boys nodded. "I imagine we are safe enough but I believe in taking all possible precautions." Picking up one of the musketoons, I continued, "are either of you familiar with the operation of one of these?' Both nodded. "Excellent," I said, "until we reach Charleston the three of us shall sleep in my cabin in shifts. Two will be sleeping while one stands guard outside the door. Agreed?" They nodded again and so it was for the brief period until we docked in Charleston.

After docking and the departure of the three mutineers I called for the Captain of the watch. When he arrived I escorted him to Jimmy's corpse and cut open the bag. The watchman smiled and pulled a folded paper out of a pocket. Handing it to me he simply said "Your lucky day sir!" When I unfolded it I saw a reasonable likeness of

Jimmy under bold type proclaiming "Prince Jimmy the scourge of the Carolinas." It offered a 300 guinea reward for his capture dead or alive. It was issued by order of Governor James Glen. I felt a hearty laugh rising in my chest.

The Artist

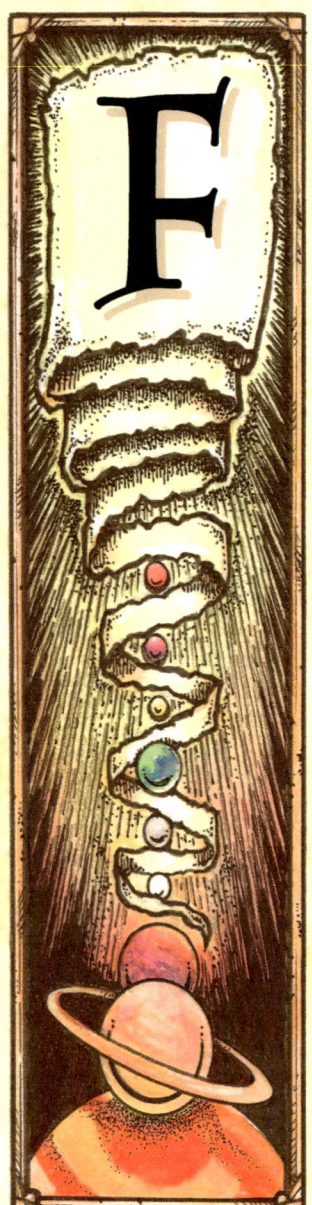

Francis lived with his family. Most of them didn't much care for his company, a feeling he reciprocated, but they did appreciate his income.

The only member of the family Francis had a good relationship with was his step-sister Jo's daughter Vivian. It was Saturday and Francis might have walked Vivian into town but Jo had taken her and the family car to run errands in a neighboring town. Francis headed to the garage where he had set up a small studio space in an unused corner. Creating drawings of imagined scenes was his passion.

Francis worked as an animator for a maker of second rate cartoons. He mostly worked on the backgrounds of the cels. It was boring work but it provided a steady income. On weekends he spent most his time in his "studio" drawing scenes out of his imagination working with colored pencils. On this day he closed the garage door and took a seat on a stool to begin work. He turned on the light and opened his 11x14 sketchbook and

looked at the picture of a dragon he'd begun last weekend. It needed something and he thought he knew what. He opened the drawer of the desk the sketchbook sat on and groaned. Most of his pencils were down to nubs. He'd forgotten that he used them nearly up last Sunday.

He closed the drawer and his sketchbook. Turning off the light he walked out of the garage and headed into town. The five and dime where he usually bought art supplies was out of the pencils he needed. The drug store had nothing but crayons. He'd have to wait for Jo to get back with the car so he started home. Just to have some different views he took a secondary street he didn't often walk along. The street was mixed residential and commercial. He saw men working on cars, beauty shops and an occasional machine shop; all with multiple houses in between. Up the road a bit he spied a storefront with an elaborately lettered old sign. As he got nearer the shop he read the sign which said "Art Supplies."

He didn't notice his pace quickening but in no time at all he was opening the door. A pleasant bell chimed as the door closed. An old man entered the front of the store from the back room "What may I help you with young man?" "Colored pencils" Francis blurted out "I need a box of new ones." The man stared Francis up and down and looked into his face for what seemed a long time before he said, "I think I have what you need. Please follow me." Francis followed him to the back counter of the store which seemed a much longer walk than he would have thought but then the old man reached up and grabbed a large shallow box, blew the dust off it and laid it on the counter. He opened the box and all other thoughts fled Francis's mind as he beheld the exquisite colors of the set before him on the counter.

He counted twenty-four pencils already sharpened to perfect points. The colors seemed to glow like jewels, each more lovely than the last. Lying in their box they struck him almost as living things. He knew he had to have them. "How much?" he asked tremulously, fearing the answer. "Well now let me see," muttered the old man. "How much do you have in your wallet?" Puzzled, Francis opened his wallet and counted "I have $44" he announced. "And in your pocket?", the old man continued. "Another 77 cents," Francis stammered. "Well," the old man stretched out the word "you're just a bit short but you seem like a fine young man so I'll let you have them for a discount." He smiled at Francis and proceeded to wrap the set up like a parcel, took every bit of Francis's money and then scooted him out of the store.

Hardly able to believe his good fortune Francis barely managed to keep himself from running all the way home. As he turned from the sidewalk into the driveway he noticed the family sedan parked in front of the garage. Vivian hurried toward him carrying a book in one hand and something that turned out to be a hat in the other. Anxious as he was to get to work Francis took a few moments to exclaim over Vivian's new acquisitions. "You'll look lovely in your new hat when I get around to sketching you," he said. "Now I need to get to work in the studio." He didn't notice Vivian blush or her stare as he walked to the garage.

He sat in the studio admiring the pencils as they were bathed in the glow from his drawing lamp. He opened the sketchbook and looked at the dragon picture. He felt it wasn't worthy of his new instruments. He closed the book and put it aside revealing a 24x36 hard bound sketchbook he'd received at Christmas had been saving ever since. He opened it to the first page and somehow, on its clean white surface he could see the picture he would create. The hero was standing by a fountain in the town square; receiving a bounty from the king amidst a throng of cheering town's people. In the middle distance another crowd of town's folk dancing around the body of a slain dragon and, in the further distance a fine castle overlooking the town. He set to work.

Hours past unnoticed as Francis worked feverishly on the scene. The picture became more and more real to him with each bit of detail he added; each subtle bit a shading to add depth to the faces. He felt as if he was being drawn into the picture he was creating. Or was he creating it? At times it felt as if he was just an instrument in some other hand. Shortly after sunset Vivian interrupted by knocking on the door and inquiring if he would be joining the family for dinner. He laughed "No, sweet heart. I am having much too much fun to quit now. I'll see you tomorrow."

And that was the last time anyone saw Francis alive. When Vivian woke up the next day she went to Francis's room to say good morning. The door stood open and the bed had clearly not been slept in. She had a bad feeling as she went to tell her mother of her discovery. At Vivian's urging Jo went out to the garage where she discovered Francis slumped over his drawing desk. During the next few hours, as Vivian sat crying in her bedroom, there was a parade of policemen, paramedics, and finally a coroner. Since no one could identify any cause of death it was classified as death by natural causes.

Throughout that day and the following weeks Vivian moved in a grey fog. Sometimes she felt sick to her stomach with sorrow. Late on that first night, when all the rest of the family was asleep she took an old box she'd got a dress in and emptied out the few items it contained. She went out to the garage and closed the sketchbook, put the pencils in their box and put both in her box which she covered and returned to its place under the bed. It was a few weeks later and her sorrow had abated to a constant dull ache when Vivian decided to pull out the box and examine the contents. When she opened the large sketchbook she gasped and a teary smile flitted across her face.

Francis's last picture was incredible. In fact, it was more like looking out through a window than looking at a picture. Right in center stood Francis in a heroic pose. Oh, he'd been idealized quite a bit but it was still obviously Francis and she felt just that little bit better for looking at it. The next day was Saturday and she made a plan. That next morning she found her savings book and put it in her

pocket. She took out the sketchbook and began the walk into town. First she stopped at the bank where she discovered she had $123.00. She withdrew $100 and proceeded to the picture framing shop. The lady at the shop said the picture could be framed for $77.35 and would be ready in three weeks. She paid the lady and left the sketchbook at the frame shop. On her way home she deposited the change back into her savings account.

It was nearly two months since Francis had passed when she brought the picture home. Her mom helped her hang it on the wall at the foot of her bed so that it could be the first and last thing she saw each day. A few days later she was lying in bed and looking at the picture when the most amazing thing happened. You might want to call it a trick of light but Vivian knew what she had seen. A super-sized smile spread over her face as she contemplated that fact that Francis (or his picture) had clearly winked at her.

The Last Freely Elected Poet Laureate

hey came for him in a small caravan of limousines. Three to be precise; gleaming white in the semi-tropical sun. He made them wait while he savored the last of his breakfast.

When their nervousness became palpable he took a final bite of toast, drained his coffee and arose to don his suit coat. Their route to the stadium was lined with cheering spectators who, being unable to obtain a ticket, wished for a glimpse of his expressionless face as the caravan passed by. Once he winked at a good looking young woman who blushed prettily. Another time he bestowed an almost undetectable smile on a little boy.

Later, at the stadium, after receiving the emblems of his office he declaimed his newest work to thunderous applause which shook the stands.

He lay back in the plush rear seat. He was too exhausted to even open his eyes as the caravan retraced its route through the cheering throngs. Back at the compound he staggered through the door and into his study. He ordered the drapes to be drawn as he fell onto the cool leather sofa. As she knelt beside him he gently brushed her cheek and shook his head. Perhaps there will be time for that later he thought. But now he must rest and collect his thoughts. Soon he would have to decide.

An hour or more passed before he was awoken by a violent thunder storm. He stood up and walked to a window to draw back the drapes. The wind toyed with the trees as the rain obscured most of his view. He felt refreshed by the brief nap and energized by the elemental display. Should he call the girl or get to his task? He paused a moment longer and then turned to his desk. As he sat down at the mahogany desk he opened the center drawer and removed a small box covered with ostrich skin. Opening the box he withdrew his favorite pen and checked to be sure its ink well was full. From a leather desktop holder he withdrew a sheet of Benneton Graveur stationery with his family crest at the top of the page and began to write.

He wrote easily in a lovely flowing cursive. Occasionally he would pause and stare off into space before he resumed his writing. After about twenty minutes the page was nearly full. He signed the bottom with a flourish, withdrew an envelope from another desktop holder and wrote "To whom it may concern" on the envelope before carefully folding the stationery and placing it in the envelope which he put at the head of the desk. Putting the pen back in its box he returned the box to the center drawer and withdrew a beautifully engraved derringer with inlaid ivory handle.

"It is all done now," he thought, "I've left nothing unsaid." He placed the barrel against the roof of his mouth. The sun broke briefly through the clouds as the man slumped on the desk. A thin trickle of blood stained the blotter.

"Truth and fantasy live together....

....in a never again to be the same way place.

Stories of the Mundane World

"Waiting for the light to dawn, passing through the dreams we sleep upon"

Cold Service

I t's no use Mr. Sampson. There was no murder. The coroner's report states quite clearly that your wife died of natural causes, as you well know." "And pray tell Detective McNaughton; precisely what natural causes were responsible for my wife's demise?"

W ell," McNaughton paused, "the coroner can't be absolutely sure but speculates that heart failure could have been the primary cause," Sampson injected a bitter laugh, "In a woman whose doctor pronounced her heart in good health two days prior, as indicated in his deposition?" McNaughton drew himself up, "Listen Sampson; there was no sign of a struggle and the "suspect" you wanted us to investigate has a solid alibi." "There was no struggle because she recovered from the flu only a few days prior, McNaughton." But Sampson was running out of steam as McNaughton was running out of patience. "Listen here Sampson, we're sympathetic to your loss but we can't have you turning up at the station every few days to hector me and my staff. The next time you show up you will be charged with disturbing the peace."

A crestfallen Sampson collected his things and departed in silence. "If I have to take matters into my own hands then so be it," he thought as he walked along, indifferent to his surroundings. He recalled the night of Marion's death. He'd been out a bit late playing chess with an old friend. He arrived home deep in thought and hadn't noticed if the door was locked. He wasn't surprised that Marion didn't reply when he called out. She'd recently been sick and had likely fallen asleep early. The first thing he noticed upon entering their bedroom was that she was on his side of the bed; next he saw that she was still wearing her dressing gown over her nightie. These were two things which hadn't happened in over twenty years of marriage. Lastly he noticed the stillness; the terrible stillness. He tried to resuscitate her but she was so limp he knew it was hopeless. He sobbed as he dialed 911 to report her death. He didn't remember most of the rest of the night except that somehow his doctor showed up and gave him a pill which briefly ended his ordeal.

In days that followed he moved in a fog until he learned that Marion's passing had been determined to be a result of her age and weakened condition. Explaining the oddity of the way he found her made no impression on the Detective assigned to the case. When he explained the motive that a substantial inheritance would be provided to her son the police grudgingly checked his whereabouts on the night in question. One of the son's female acquaintances swore they'd been together the whole night. When pressed she allowed as how she had slept soundly that night but she swore that she would have awoke if he had departed and returned. The police were satisfied. Likewise, Marion's doctor's deposition affirming her heart's good health had made no impression on the authorities. "Well," Sampson thought, "he knew what he knew and he would ensure that justice was done."

A week passed during which he contracted a cold; complete with a stuffy nose and sore throat. He was lying propped up in bed reading and sucking on a lozenge when he was hit with a particularly violent coughing fit. When he realized he was about to swallow the lozenge he managed to roll to his hands and knees where he was able to cough out the lozenge. As he lay back down he congratulaed himself on saving his own life with his quick thinking. As the minutes passed a devious plan began to form in his mind. "The question," he thought, "was whether he was willing to sacrifice so much in order to avenge his wife's murder?" He decided to give the matter more thought as he turned out the bedside lamp and closed his eyes.

A few days later, having answered his question in the affirmative, he was out shopping for hard candies and cough drops.

He had also purchased a funnel which narrowed to a little less than an inch. When he got home he began testing the ability of the candies or cough drops to pass through the funnel. When he was done he had four candies and one cough drop. He put the rest in a bag for later disposal. He ran the hot water in the kitchen sink and adjusted it until it was as hot as he could stand to drink. One by one he placed the lozenges in the funnel and poured the hot water on top. He found he could hold about three ounces in his mouth so that was the amount he poured on top of each lozenge. Not surprisingly, the cough drop dissolved the quickest. At about two and one-half minutes it fell through the funnel along with the remaining water. He was now ready to begin his final preparations.

First, he pulled out one unused cough drop and unwrapped it. He put the wrapper and the funnel in the bag with the unused candies and their wrappers. It was late afternoon when he took a short walk to the neighborhood park. No one was about as he dropped the bag into a trash receptacle. He went home and wrote a brief note detailing his suspicions of his stepson Ralph and stating his fear that his stepson might kill him in order to become the executor of his mother's will. He folded the paper, placed it into an envelope and wrote "In the Event of my Death" on one side. He placed that envelope inside the pillow cover of his pillow so that his head would rest upon it. He found a post card Ralph had sent to Marion and spent several hours practicing his stepson's poor penmanship. He found a copy of his will and, doing his best to copy Ralph's style he wrote a codicil stating that his stepson should be his sole beneficiary.

He had been sleeping in the guest room since Marions death. He put the unwrapped cough drop on the night stand in the guest room along with an empty glass. He hadn't entered their bedroom since her death but now he picked up the second pillow from the guest bed and carried it into their room. Fortunately, all the bedding for both bedrooms was identical, having been purchased at the same time. It was hard to bear but he picked up what had been his pillow by one corner and replaced it with the one from the guest room. The one he took from their room was placed on his bed in the guest room. Since her head had rested on the other pillow he guessed that it was his pillow that Ralph had used to smother her. Perhaps they might find some trace DNA on the pillow.

He wanted to create the impression that he was not depressed so he dressed up in a good suit and went out for a fine dinner at nearby restaurant that had been one of their favorites. He hadn't been there since her death so he was required to gracefully accept the condolences of the owner, the maître d and their usual waiter. He forced himself to smile appreciatively as the waiter shared a fond memory with the delivery of each course. His meal completed, he thanked them all once again and assured them that he'd be back.

At home he carefully returned his clothing to the closet or the hamper and slipped into his pajamas. The front of the house was darkened as he opened the door part way and slid the small oval rug against the door. He hoped it would prevent the door from opening until pushed. He had wiped the knob on both sides with a kleenex he deposited in the bathroom waste basket. He took the glass from the night table and filled it with hot water knowing it would cool a bit before he needed it. Back in the guest room he set down the glass and arranged his pillow to keep his head

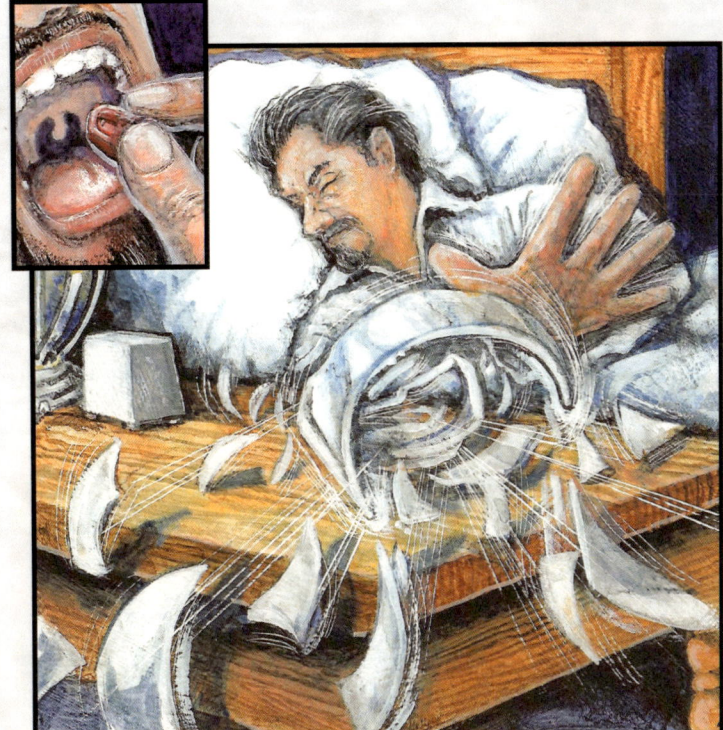

A wind strong enough to blow the front door open came up just before dawn so when the neighborhood gossip looked out that morning she saw it was wide open. She called 911 and a patrol car showed up in minutes. A few minutes later Detective McNaughton showed up and an hour after that the coroner. The same dullness and lack of imagination that had infuriated Sampson before now served him well. All the clues were discovered and read exactly as hoped. Ralph protested mightily but hadn't known he'd need an alibi and had none. The lack of finger prints on the front door knob was certainly suspicious. The last straw was the discovery of Ralph's trace DNA on the pillowcase.

propped up and looking at the ceiling. He got into bed and once under the covers began to thrash about, hoping to create the impression of a struggle. He sat up in bed, placed the cough drop in his mouth and swallowed. He felt it stick somewhere in the vicinity of his esophagus. When he began to feel faint he took a swallow of the still very warm water. He missed the table when he tried to set the glass down and heard a crash as he laid his head down on the pillow. His last thought was that the broken glass would be a fine addition to the crime scene. As his muscles relaxed the water washed what was left of the lozenge into his stomach where it dissolved in the remains of his last supper.

Lost

Eleanor was driving the rental car south through West Virginia. Beside her was her current boyfriend William. He was reasonably attractive with a good sense of humor. Their tastes in movies and music had proven to be fairly compatible.

They'd been dating for a few weeks and had decided to take a short road trip. It was an experiment that would determine what next steps might happen, if any. They'd reserved an Airbnb, significantly it had two bedrooms. Neither of them wanted the pressure of having to share a bed. They were still about two hours from their destination when William asked her to pull over. Before she could ask him why she'd had to pull over he pointed to sign announcing a scenic overlook of an entire valley. "That sounds cool" he said "want to check it out?" Eleanor checked the car's clock and saw they had plenty of time. She smiled at William, put the car in gear and followed the turn off. When they got to the parking lot they saw a sign stating they were at a trail head. It informed that the hike to the overlook was 1.3 miles and of moderate difficulty.

It was mid-afternoon on a warm fall day. The leaves were turning and there were still a few hours before sunset so they decided to go for it. Eleanor texted their host that they might be a little late. She grabbed her small backpack because she always had some water bottles in it along with other odds and ends. They started down the path in high spirits. They were a little more than half way to the overlook when they heard a low growl off to their right. They looked in the direction the sound came and spotted a black bear in a tree about 200 feet away. Without warning William panicked and started running in the opposite direction. After a brief hesitation Eleanor set off after him. She began calling for him to stop but it was to no avail.

After about five or so minutes he began to slow down and finally sank to the ground by the trunk of a downed yellow poplar. Eleanor noticed that his breath was ragged as she took a seat on the tree trunk. As she waited for William to regain his composure Eleanor checked her watch and noted they had about two hours of daylight. The sky was overcast so there was no way to guess directions from the sun's position. She stood up and surveyed the forest doing a complete 360. The view was nearly identical in every direction. The area they were in had a consistent gentle slope but as she looked further down the slope it led to another rise. There was no way around it…they were lost.

Wat are we going to do?" William blurted out. Eleanor was annoyed by the plaintive tone of the query but decided to ignore that. "We're going to look for an animal trail and follow it" she said in a calm voice. "How?" was all that William had to say. It was clear to Eleanor that she was in charge. "You are going to stay right where you are. I will walk in a circle around you looking for signs of a trail. After I complete each circle I'll walk a little further away from you and circle around again. Hopefully I'll come across a trail before you're out of sight." William said nothing but he did get up off the ground and sit on the tree. As she took her first step away from him he offered a wan smile and said "Don't get lost." She returned his smile and began walking.

Forty-five minutes later William was still visible but he was about 200 feet away. She was about to step in some deer scat but saw it just in time. She stopped and examined the ground. There was a narrow faint depression heading into some shrubbery. Examining the bushes she noticed a few broken branches at the side of the depression. Convinced she was standing on a trail she called William to join her. The terrain was flat so she mentally tossed a coin as he made his way to where she was standing. She pointed out the evidence to William and pointed toward the gap in the bushes. "We'll go that way."

After following the trail for about 30 minutes the light began to dim. Eleanor began looking for a spot to spend the night. 20 minutes later she felt rather than saw the beginning of a gentle down slope. Then she noticed a ring of shrubbery that had an opening in the middle. She stopped and turned around to face William. Pointing to the shrubs she said "We'll sleep here." She shrugged off her backpack, opened it up and started to rummage through the contents. As she did that William spied an energy bar, said "Food!" and started reaching for the backpack. Eleanor pulled it way, aimed a disarming smile at William and said, "We've got a few chores to complete before dinner. "

She pulled a multi-tool out of the pack, closed it and slipped it back over her shoulders. "We have about twenty minutes before twilight. Collect as many leaves as you can from the ground here and I'll trim some branches. Between the two we'll have a softer bed than this hard ground." William looked a bit disgruntled but turned to his task. When sun dipped behind the horizon they had assembled a bed leaves and branches about 8 inches high. Eleanor pulled a folded up rain poncho out of her pack and together they placed it over the pile. A few more minutes and they had a pile of rocks at each corner. They sat down on their "mattress" facing each other. She opened the backpack and pulled out an energy bar, "We have no idea how long we'll be out in the woods so we must conserve our resources". She unwrapped the bar, pulled out the multi-tool and opened the blade. After cutting the bar into two unequal pieces she handed him the larger piece. "Take your time she suggested," as he took in half his piece in one bite. She shook her head, took a tiny bite and said, "Suit yourself." After "dinner" was consumed she pulled out a 16 oz. bottle of water and then a small collapsible cup. She opened the cup and poured about 4 oz. of water into it. William quickly drained the cup and handed it back to her. She poured a like amount into the cup and took her time sipping it.

Night had fallen and the only illumination was from stars and a waning moon. Eleanor put her things, including the wrapper back into her pack and zipped it closed. She arranged the pack so she could use it as a pillow. She laid down saying "Goodnight," an utterance that went unanswered. Reviewing the day while staring at the night sky Eleanor rapidly concluded that William was not at all who she'd hoped. Assuming they found their way back without too much trouble she would have to count the experience as her good fortune for exposing William's shortcomings. Her last thought was of the beauty of the night sky.

She woke a little before dawn. She pulled out another energy bar, hoping they wouldn't need the last one. Dividing the bar as before she took out the water bottle and cup. She poured some water into the cup and poked William until he stirred. "What time is it he said with a resentful tone." "Time for breakfast" she answered and handed him the piece of energy bar. When he'd finished it she handed him the water bottle as she interspersed sips from the glass with tiny bites. When she finished she packed up glass and the wrapper, stood up and began tugging at the poncho. William slowly stood up and she stuffed the poncho into her pack. She slipped the pack over her shoulder and said, "Time to get going."

After walking along the animal track for about an hour the sun began to crest the ridge to the east. The path continued to gently descend. After walking for another 30 minutes or so Eleanor caught sight of a bright flash a few hundred feet to her right. She stopped and pondered the sight. She could think of nothing natural that would produce such a flash when struck by the sun. "Follow me," she said and without looking back began walking toward flash of light. The flash began to dim as the sun continued to rise but remained visible until she stopped within a couple of hundred feet of the object and began to laugh. Her laugh conveyed both amusement and relief. "What is it?" William asked her. In answer she pulled the keys out of her pocket and pressed the fob. A couple of hundred feet away a horn sounded and headlights flashed.

Dreamer

The oversized porch glider moved slowly in the flower scented breeze. It was large enough for him to lie prone, if he bent his knees, with his head in her lap.

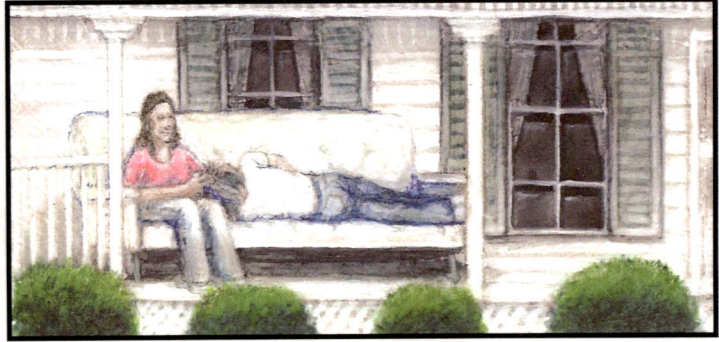

His puzzlement was like small lightning fast mosquito trying to penetrate their air of contentment. "But why," he asked "should a beautiful, intelligent and assertive woman, who is so much younger than myself, want to attach herself to a withered old prune like me?"

She smiled down at him as she pushed off the floor with one foot to keep the glider in motion. Then she looked across the yard and above the garden shrubbery to the distant mountains. "That's an easy thing to know and yet quite difficult to express," she replied. "Think of it this way.

People will often suggest that their lover completes them; but no one can complete another." She paused and began again, "I am able to complete myself more easily in your presence. You don't do it but you enable it"

Can't you be any more specific than that?" he asked and she began to laugh. "Get your lazy butt up off the seat, go in the house and fetch some cheeses and a brite bottle of wine. "Perhaps I'll have more to say when you return" she said, giving him a gentle shove.

She let her mind drift as she glided back and forth, listening to the sounds coming out of the kitchen. She heard his footsteps on the porch and opened her eyes. He set the cork tray on the glider seat so it was in between them. Two stemless glasses filled nearly to the rim with yellow tinged liquid sat admist a narrow plate containing several soft and hard cheeses, a bowl of olives and some slices of baguette.

"This looks just right," she said as she popped an olive in her mouth while placing a slice of cheese on a piece of bread. "I've thought about your question and I do have a bit more to say." A smile lit her eyes as she spoke. "But first, you must make an effort to explain your presence here; an outcome that you resisted mightily as I recall. I won't be the only one doing the heavy lifting."

He assumed a thoughtful frown, looked up to the heavens and sighed. She responded with what was nearly a belly laugh, "You won't avoid your share that easily." "I suppose I wanted to be courted," he said, "and, to be frank, I didn't believe that I deserved you." he took a sip of wine, passed her a shy look and continued, "a doubt I'm still not able to completely vanquish."

Why am I here, you've asked," he touched her cheek. "Is it enough to say that I am totally and unalterably seduced?" He laughed and answered his question, "no, I suppose not." Let me say that with all the fine moments, exciting and passionate moments you have gifted me with it is the serenity of my life with you; all those moments and even the occasional angry or sad moments…they all seem to be set within some realm of infinite peace." The depth he saw in her eyes as he concluded stopped him. "I'm afraid that's the best I can offer," he said with a self-deprecating smile. They sat in companionable silence, enjoying their repast, as the sun drifted nearer the horizon heralding the coming twilight. Finally he broke the silence "I'll have the rest of my answer now. If you feel I've earned it."

She pulled his hand to her face, kissing it and then holding it to her cheek for so long he wondered if she might not answer. Then, watching intently, he realized she was about to begin. "More specifically," she smiled, "your sense of humor is very endearing." As she spoke he heard in the distance an approaching siren. "I find the way you can infuse appropriate humor into virtually any interaction brilliant." The siren was growing louder as it was getting nearer making making concentration hard for him "Could you repeat that?" he asked, as the noise came to a crescendo and the scene began to dissolve.

His eyes opened upon a flat white ceiling and he wept silently as he rolled onto his side and reached for the alarm clock. Yet through the tears a keen observer have might detected, as he fell back, a very faint hint of a smile.

illard's attention was divided as he drove along a country road flanked by fields of corn high enough to prevent him seeing anything other than corn and road. He was in one of the fly over states in the central plains of the United States.

Being on such a stretch of road made it easier for him to devote a substantial part of attention to his contemplation of his future. Willard was a watchmaker, although, in truth, he mostly did repair, cleaning and appraisals. In fact, he was on his way to a client's farm to appraise some watches as he considered his prospects. He hoped the items would be valuable enough to earn some breathing room in his budget for a month or two. He was a good ten years away from being able to collect social security and hadn't saved much for retirement. He worked out of his house which he owned outright so his modest life style didn't require a large cash flow. Still, the income produced by his business had been in steady decline for the past few decades, a trend that would surely continue.

It started back when digital watches first appeared. They were reliable and cheap enough to throw out and replace if they stopped working. The amount he made selling them barely covered his morning coffee and a sweet roll. Folks in farming country were mostly frugal but he still managed to sell an occasional Omega or Waltham and folks who had good quality watches still invested in cleaning and maintenance. He limped along until the advent of smart watches. His sales dropped to nothing as they became increasingly common. Cleaning and repair jobs were becoming much more infrequent. How long would it be before he needed to find a new job; and what might that be.

Willard's musings were interrupted as he came around a gentle bend in the road to see an ancient truck parked on the shoulder of the road with the hood up. The man standing beside the truck looked at least as ancient as the truck. He was waving a red handkerchief in an apparent effort to flag Willard down. Willard waved at the man as he passed the truck and pulled his car over onto the shoulder.

Willard felt his shirt plaster itself to his body as he turned off the car and got out. The man walking toward him appeared to be north of eighty, maybe even north of 90. "Can I help you?" Willard asked. "Are you an auto mechanic?" the man responded in a disgusted tone. "I'm afraid not," Willard replied, "but I could call for service or give you a ride," as he pulled his smart phone out of his pocket. The old man cracked small grin as his eye fell on Willard's 5 year old sedan. "Figures that a guy with such a new car would have one of them expensive high tech phones".

Willard responded with a tight smile. He held up his phone and repeated is initial question "Can I help you?" The old man paused putting his hand to his forehead. "It would be helpful if you could call Frank's Automotive Service for me." Before Willard could initiate a search the old man rapidly rattled of the number and then slowly repeated it. Willard punched in the number and handed the phone to the old man. After a short wait the old man began speaking "Hello Marjorie, it's me Arnold…yup, the truck broke down again…what! You can tell where I am from the phone? Never thought I'd see the day…about 20 minutes… okay." Arnold handed the phone back to Willard, who terminated the call.

Putting the phone back in his pocket Willard spoke, "Well, I guess I'd better get going now." Arnold mumbled something while staring at the ground. "What's that you say Arnold?" Arnold looked up with a hint of a blush and blurted out "I got to get home and take care of the livestock." Willard looked at him and asked "Can't the tow truck driver give you ride?" Arnold shook his head and said "I'm in the opposite direction so he'll take me into town and I won't get a ride home until they close up. Be pretty late by then."

How far is it your house?" Willard asked. "About twenty minutes," was the reply. Willard sighed and pulled his phone back out. "I'll have to reschedule an appointment I was driving to". He brought up the contact and hit call icon. "Hello Mr. Sumner…yes I've been delayed…you have another appointment…can we reschedule?" Willard was annoyed as he noticed the satisfied smile on Arnolds face. "Okay sir, I'll call next week." Arnold mumbled something again and Willard was forced to ask what he'd said. "I said I'm sorry about disrupting your business." "It can't be helped," Willard offered as he peered down the road hoping to see a tow truck.

Thirty minutes later Willard and Arnold were driving down a dirt road. "How much further to your farm?" Willard asked. Arnold smiled and said, "we've been on it for the last five minutes. The house is just ahead on the right." Willard spied a two-track on the right a few minutes later and turned onto it. In another few minutes he pulled up to a nondescript box of a farm house. As he turned to Arnold the old man thanked him and asked if he had a business card. Willard pulled out his wallet, extracted a card and handed it to Arnold. "A watchmaker, heh?" Arnold said. "Perhaps I'll have some work for you in the future." The old man got out; they said their farewells and Willard's old sedan disappeared down the driveway. He shook his head thinking about the querulous old man as he turned onto the road. It was the last time he thought of him.

It was early the following spring and Willard was cleaning house. His business had continued to decline over the fall and he had stopped buying new stock. He let all of his subscriptions lapse except for the Horological Times. He stopped that final subscription during the winter as his diet became restricted to day old goods and manager's specials. A few weeks ago he'd sold the last of his stock. He was expecting a workman to come for the display cabinets he'd

sold anytime now. Tomorrow he would list the house for sale. He was hopeful that the money from house, his increasingly frugal life style and perhaps some part-time work would allow him to survive until social security kicked in.

At the ring of the doorbell he opened the door. Instead of the workman he was expecting he saw an obviously prosperous gentleman in a rather expensive suit. "Can I help you sir?" said the puzzled watchmaker. "Are you Willard Swenson, the watchmaker?" the gentleman enquired. "Yes sir, but I'm no longer in the business." The gentleman handed Willard a card "I'm not here on business," he smiled, "at least not that sort." Willard read the card which stated the man was an attorney specializing in wills and probate. He went on "I'm handling the estate of Arnold Weathersby." Willard racked his brain "Was he a crotchety old man with a pick-up that belonged in a junk yard?" Willard asked.

The attorney laughed "Arnold would have endorsed that description. May I come in?" Willard ushered the attorney in and led him to the dining room table. After placing his brief case on the table he opened it and spoke again. "Arnold asked me to convey to you his gratitude for your kind assistance and to give you this" The attorney pulled an old Crown Royal bag out of the brief case and handed it to Willard. As he took the bag he was surprised by the weight of its contents. Still confused he opened the bag and saw a watch case. His heart began to race as he pulled it out noting its obvious age and the logo of Patek Philippe. His hand was shaking as he opened the case. His legs nearly failed him and he sank into a dining room chair as he beheld the contents.

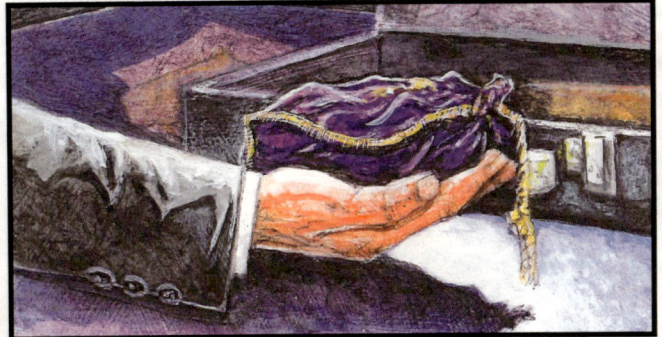

There lay an untouched Patek Philippe model 3448 Automatic Perpetual Calendar. He remained speechless as the attorney handed him an envelope "The bill of sale, the accompanying certificate and a recent appraisal," the attorney explained as he closed his brief case and headed for the door. "I don't understand" – "Willard whispered as the attorney reached the door. The attorney turned and spoke. "Arnold left you this in his will. Any taxes due have been paid. Good day sir." With that the attorney was gone. Willard knew the value could well be somewhere in seven figures but when he pulled the appraisal out and read the amount he began to weep, even as a large smile formed on his face.

To have said that the bedding was rumpled would have been a vast understatement. The blanket and top sheet had fallen off and lay on either side of the bed. The fitted sheet needed fitting.

They lay on their sides facing each other and she wondered aloud if her face had as goofy a smile pasted on it as his did. He assured her that was the case.

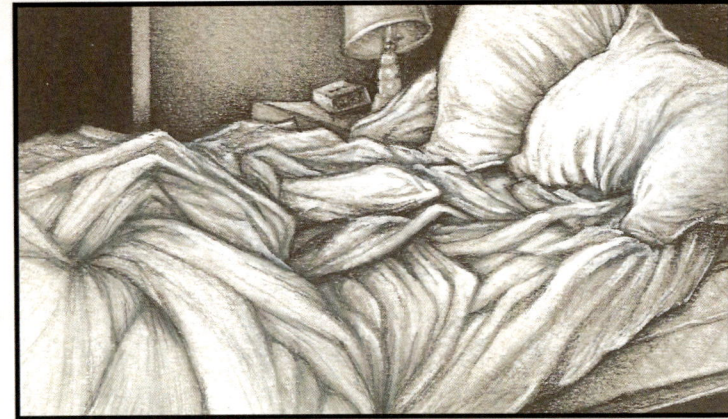

She closed her eyes and thought back a few hours to when she heard a vaguely familiar voice call her name. She placed the last grocery bag and closed the trunk. Turning around she saw one of her neighbors; Roger? Yes Roger and Christine. They had been friendly, but never really friends.

"Hello Roger. What's up?" "Nothing much" he replied "I just wanted to say hello, see how you're doing." She stared at him without immediately responding. It seemed too personal a question coming from a casual acquaintance.

So how are you doing? I guess it's a little awkward but I'm wondering because," he paused to look down and then up again, "Christine moved out three months ago; it seems like the life I thought I had is gone. There are all these voids." He stopped as a hint of a blush began to form "I'm sorry, it's presumptuous of me. Please accept my apology." As he turned and took a step she found herself saying "It does get better, but only bit by bit." He turned back and gave her such a hopeful look that she had to smile. "Would you like to come over? I'll make a pot of coffee and we can talk for a while." "I know the way," he nodded and headed for his car.

Her mind was racing as she drove home "What if I've misjudged him?" she thought; then, "he's not bad looking, seems to be in good condition," then, "what the hell am I doing?" And then she was home. She opened the trunk, grabbed the bag of groceries, and headed for the door as he pulled up in front of the house. He grabbed a couple of bags from the trunk and headed toward her as she got the door open and entered the house. He followed her into the kitchen, set the bags down on the counter and headed back out "I'll get the last bags while you start putting stuff away." She closed the freezer door and started on a pot of coffee as he set the last of the groceries down. He leaned on the counter and watched her start the coffee "Suddenly I'm not getting invited to neighborhood get-togethers where I used to be a regular," he shook his head. She couldn't help letting out a bitter laugh, "you never noticed when I stopped showing up?" "Oh! How could I have been so stupid?" he slapped his forehead, "I thought you just didn't feel like socializing." "Couples groups aren't fond of singles," she muttered, "and my few remaining friends don't live nearby." They continued talking along this line and after a bit she looked at the clock and declared, "its afternoon. I say we should switch to wine." She put the coffee cups in the sink and replaced them with two wine glasses. Pouring red wine into each about half way up she picked up one. "A toast, to surviving."

After another 30 minutes or so of conversation Roger stood up "I sure appreciate this time we've spent together. I have only one more thing to ask, if it's not to forward, I could really use a hug before I go." She got up and they hugged. The hug went on for quite a while and she realized she was liking it. Something stirred within her and, she noticed, in him too. She let her arms drop down to the small of his back, looked up and spoke "It's funny, but I never quit" she smiled at his quizzical expression "taking the birth control pills." She kissed him, took his hand and led him to the bedroom.

As she was contemplating the course of the day she realized he had spoken "What did you say?" "That had to be the world's best ever hug," he repeated and they giggled. She heard the front door open and blurted out "Eva!" "Daughter?" he asked. She nodded, pointed at him, his clothes on the floor and the bathroom door. While he collected the clothes and slid into the bathroom she piled her clothes and the bedding on the bed. She just managed to close the robe she'd slipped into when Eva appeared in the doorway. She surveyed the scene, sniffed the air and with a loud "eww!" she turned on her heel and walked back toward the kitchen. "I'll be in my room," she said as she disappeared around a corner. The bathroom door opened as the bedroom door closed. They looked at each other and burst out laughing.

Old Man

He lay in the ancient bed, the room dimly lit by a night light in the adjoining bathroom. His eyes were closed but he was awake and thinking "Is this the day I fail to rise from my bed?"

He started counting all his aching body parts but got disgusted and quit at 10, when he hadn't even got to his hips. Outside there was the faintest hint of light in the eastern sky and the earliest birds began their incessant conversations. The man sighed and threw back the covers.

He rolled to the edge of the bed and managed to force himself into a sitting position. After a short trip to the bathroom he slipped on a robe and sat at his desk watching the sunrise. "It's a school day," he thought, "the boy will be stopping by." He smiled at that thought as he got up and went to his closet. By the time the late spring sun had crested the horizon he was dressed and preparing a small breakfast. A little after eight there was a quiet knock on the door.

I can't even shout 'come in' loud enough to be heard outside" he thought as he crossed to the entry and opened the door. "Good morning, young man," was quickly answered by "Good morning sir," as the boy slipped past him, picked up the battered travel size guitar and sat on the bench facing the music stand. The man listened, pleased, as the boy began practicing scales.

He remembered how it had started on a warm day last fall with him sitting on the front patio playing a few old tunes. The boy stopped on the sidewalk and listened until the man invited him into the patio. He listened to another song and asked, "Do you think I could learn to do that?" Smiling, the old man had said, "I'm sure of it. Why don't you ask your parents send you to a teacher?" The boy shook his head and said "We don't have money for that kind of thing." The man had invited the boy into his house and handed him the old travel guitar. He showed him three chords and they played a song together. It was getting late and boy said, "I better go or I'll be in trouble when I get home." The old man went to a book shelf and pulled out a beginning guitar book. "Take this with you and study the finger positions. Anytime you want to bring it back you can practice on the guitar; either on your way to school or on your way home." The boy took the book and put it in his back pack. He smiled, said "see you tomorrow" and was gone. And so, twice on nearly every school day since came the knock on his door. The boy would practice for about twenty minutes and leave.

He is getting better" the old man thought, "but in a few weeks it will be summer break and after that he'll be changing schools. The boy replaced the guitar, picked up his back pack and said, "see you this afternoon." The old man sat down to think. "If they can't afford lessons they certainly can't afford to buy him a guitar," he thought, "But I have more than I need." He got excited as he headed for the study. He pulled a hard guitar case out of the closet, set it on the couch and opened it revealing his thirty year old Martin. "This needs to be cleaned and restrung, "he thought."

He found the polish, a soft cloth and a new set of strings in his desk. He took

the old strings off and began to polish the guitar. He hummed softly as he stroked the guitar's body, much as a man touches a woman he loves. When guitar was buffed and beautiful he put on the new strings, tuned them and replaced the guitar in its case. "A guitar is a good thing," he said to himself, "but he'll still need lessons." He replaced the guitar in the closet and drove over to the local music store. He wrote a check for a gift certificate for six months of weekly lessons. When he got home he put the certificate in the guitar case along with a tuner and some picks. He put the guitar away with a smile.

They continued with their routine until the end of May with the end of the school year drawing near. In the afternoon of the last school day the boy's heart was heavy "I'm going to miss playing the guitar." He looked up to see the old man smiling. "Let me give you a ride home today," said the old man who had placed the Martin in the trunk. At the boy's home the old man pulled the guitar case out of the trunk and took it in the house where the boy's mother waited. He laid it on the couch and opened it "This is for your son. He has ability and passion for the guitar and he should continue to learn." He produced the certificate and said "This will allow him have six months of weekly lessons." The mother was grateful and the boy was so excited he barely noticed the old man leaving. Just a quick hug before he started playing the guitar. The old man was both happy and sad, knowing the boy would continue to grow but that he would not be seeing him

as often. As he lay in his bed that night he felt more at peace than he had for many years. He felt fulfilled and he smiled as he thought, "perhaps tonight I will have sweet dreams."

The Immaculate One

Gary Butler, AKA "The Immaculate One" wanted out. He was tired of the fraud his life had become. Tired of the trappings of wealth he lived with as a result of a successful fraud.

He was tired of always acting like and being treated like someone he most definitely was not. But he wasn't sure his partner would be willing to let him go. He understood that and had been working on his plan now for some months.

It had all started just a few years back with a book of inspirational poems he wrote; one for each day of the month. It was a bit quirky in that he used humor make his points. He self-published on the internet and became a minor sensation. One of the big publishing houses signed him to a contract, pulled it off line and issued a hard cover edition which took off. It climbed into the top twenty on the New York Times' list of Best Selling Non-fiction. They assigned him a booking agent and for the majority of a year he was busy on the talk show circuit, along with a few bookings for college lectures.

As soon as the bookings began to slow down his booking agent approached him with an idea that, at first, seemed crazy. They would publish a few more daily books together shifting the tone gradually toward the spiritual while still retaining a bit of humor. He would have to grow his hair long and add a good beard. The idea was to build him into a cult figure so they could profit not only on the books but t-shirts, wall art, devotional meetings, etc. With no idea what to expect he agreed to give it a try.

They had started slow but to his lasting surprise the plan worked. They began to tour the country giving lectures in small rental halls where the income from ticket sales and other merchandise only slightly exceeded the costs, but by the end of the first year he was filling public venues that could seat a thousand or more. His partner Frank wrote scripts for him to perform that he would edit to insert some of the self-deprecating humor which had made his first book a success. By the end of the second year he was appearing as "The Immaculate One" in halls holding several thousand

and money was rolling in. Early on Frank set them up as a non-profit and while most of the money went into the non-profit accounts they each received a substantial monthly stipend. Those payments added up quickly since virtually all their expenses were paid for by the non-profit.

ow Gary was anxious to quit the charade. He looked at the upcoming schedule. In two weeks they would arrive in New Orleans for two shows but there would be a couple of open days before the first one. On a free day last week he had used an internet enabled computer at a local library to check his private account which held his earnings from his first book. He noted there was still money coming in but the amounts had fallen to a couple of thousand a month at best. He'd kept up with the taxes but his nest egg was still near a quarter of a million. He had about $50K sitting in the account where his monthly stipend was deposited. He didn't want to alert Frank so he planned to transfer as much as he could late in the day before the first show in New Orleans. The next day he would arrange to transfer smaller amounts to several banks along the route he would take when he departed.

arly on the morning of the first scheduled "lesson" he filled a back pack he'd purchased the day before with a couple of changes of clothes and a bathroom kit. He managed to leave the hotel without checking out or being seen by any of the staff. He walked a few blocks to a taxi stand and caught a cab to a nearby barber shop.

The barber did as Gary asked and shaved and polished his head. His beard went next and his bushy eye brows were neatly trimmed. He caught another cab at a taxi stand down the block. He gave the driver the address of a costume shop he had found on the internet. He had called ahead and knew the shop had what he wanted in stock. At the store he took off his shirt and retrieved the cash he would need from his money belt.

fter paying the proprietor he was fitted with a fake stomach which added about fifty pounds to his apparent weight. The shop owner pulled a worn oversized Saints shirt from a rack and helped him put it on. Finally the owner used a combination of make-up and a small prosthetic to give him a double chin. He left the shop satisfied that no one could possibly recognize him. He then went to a nearby library where he got on a computer and arranged the bank transfers he thought he needed to make at the last moment to disguise his intent.

y now it was early afternoon and he was quite hungry. He stopped at the first place he saw and ordered a bowl of gumbo. He ate it with both relish and great caution so as not to disturb his extra chin. He still had some time to kill before he could board The Sunset Limited" heading west so he started walking and before he knew it he was standing across the street from the theater where he was to have spoken that night. He was greatly surprised to see the show was still listed on the marquee of the theater. In fact, his curiosity was so aroused that he resolved to take the next train tomorrow so he could see what would happen at the evening "lesson."

He found an acceptable hotel with rooms available several blocks away in the direction of the train station. Once he was checked in he lay down for a short nap. He awoke around sunset and ordered a light meal from room service. Twilight was fading from the sky when he finished supper. He left the back pack in his room and began the walk to the theater. He arrived a few minutes late and the talk was already underway. He purchased a ticket at the booth and entered the building. In the lobby he surrendered his ticket to member of what had once been his staff. He was very gratified that

the fellow showed no signs of recognition as he tore the ticket in half and returned a portion.

Gary entered the auditorium and stood in the back while his eyes adapted to the dimmed house lights. The energy in the hall reminded him of some of his better performances but it seemed to have more depth. The public address system introduced just enough distortion to make the voice hard to identify. He felt drawn to the stage. He progressed down a crowded aisle until he found himself at the edge of a group of people standing in what would serve as the orchestra pit for a stage production. He could go no further but he was close enough to recognize the speaker as his partner Frank. With hair extensions and a movie quality fake beard he looked enough like Gary had that no one was likely to notice.

As he stood there pondering what was happening Frank told his audience that he would resume shortly. He took several steps towards the end of the stage and pointed a finger at Gary. Once he could see that Gary had noticed he crooked his finger as if to call Gary to him. The human barricade between Gary and the stage parted and once again he found himself drawn closer. When he reached the stage Frank leaned over and with a twinkle in his eye he reached out his hand to Gary.

As their hands touched Gary felt warmth emanating from his hand and into the rest of his body. Muscles he hadn't realized were tense all relaxed and he felt light, though not at all light headed. The Immaculate One smiled as he released his hand. He returned to the podium and recommenced speaking as if nothing had happened. Gary turned from the

stage and headed for an exit. As he walked across the pit and up the aisle people stepped out of his way. As he reached the exit he began to consider what had just happened. "The decision I made was clearly not only good for me" he thought as he stepped out into the night.

What Dreams May Come

It had been several weeks since she had left him. That's how it felt although in truth she had succumbed after decades of struggle against the disease that she had fought off again and again.

He once again fell asleep in a miasma of grief which the alcohol could thin but not dispel. His sleep was light, restless and interspersed with periods of near wakefulness when his loss threatened to overwhelm him. Finally, with only a few hours left before dawn, he fell into a deep sleep.

In the dream they sat together on the porch of the lake house with the windows open to admit the late afternoon's cooling breezes; just as they had sat a few hundred times before. "It's so peaceful here," she sighed. "Here at the lake house?" he said with a question in his voice. "Like there," she said. As he took a sip of his bourbon and noticed she hadn't touched her brandy and water. And another thing, the Shih Tzu that usually appropriated her lap was instead curled up at her feet.

At that point in the dream he remembered that she was dead; and yet here they were sharing one of their treasured rituals in one of their treasured places. He didn't want to take a chance on disturbing or ending this dream and so he resumed surveying the lake and sipping on his bourbon. "Is it like this in any other ways?" he asked. After a brief pause she answered, "the beauty of the place is similar, but without the sense of impermanence." He thought about that as the light began to leak out of the sky and the twilight birds began to warm up for their performances.

Sitting there, looking at the lake he was experiencing the first moments of peace since she had passed. Somehow he knew it couldn't last much longer and, in fact, might not ever happen again. He had to speak "You must know that having you in my life was at the center of every truly good thing that ever happened to me." She stood up and her voice grew fainter to him, though still clear, as she said "I always knew what I meant to you and after this it should be clear to you that you meant every bit as much to me." He turned to look at her but the porch was empty and he was alone.

The sound of the early song birds woke him that morning but he remained in bed with his eyes closed for a long time. His dream remained vivid in his mind. He stayed there until he heard his granddaughter approaching. She was singing "Breakfast time. It's breakfast time." He smiled, opened his eyes, pulled back the covers and rejoined the world of the living.

"Truth and fantasy live forever!"